THIS BOOK BELONGS TO

S0-AEL-446

For Eloise —LB
For Helen and Helen —RLO

For Emily —David O'Connell

[Imprint]

A part of Macmillan Publishing Group, LLC
120 Broadway, New York, NY 10271

Library of Congress Control Number: 2019949436

ISBN 978-1-250-25634-8 (hardcover) / ISBN 978-1-250-25635-5 (ebook)

Our books may be purchased in bulk for promotional, educational, or business use.
Please contact your local bookseller or the Macmillan Corporate and Premium Sales Department at
(800) 221-7945 ext. 5442 or by email at MacmillanSpecialMarkets@macmillan.com.

Book design by Lizzie Gardiner

Special thanks to Liz Bankes and Rebecca Lewis-Oakes

Imprint logo designed by Amanda Spielman

Originally published in Great Britain by Egmont UK Limited in 2019

First American edition, 2020

1 3 5 7 9 10 8 6 4 2

mackids.com

Books are special, books are smart;
Their words are poetry, their pictures art.
So if this book be stolen, or its pages torn,
The culprit shall never in their life see a unicorn!

DAVE THE UNICORN

WELCOME TO UNICORN SCHOOL

PIP BIRD

ILLUSTRATED BY DAVID O'CONNELL

[Imprint]
MAKE YOUR MARK
New York

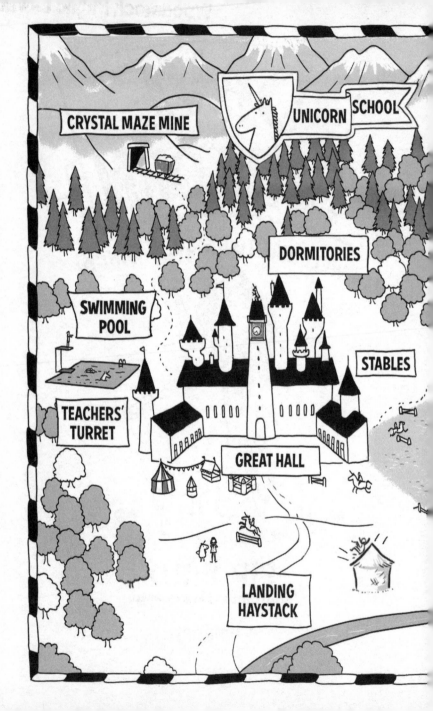

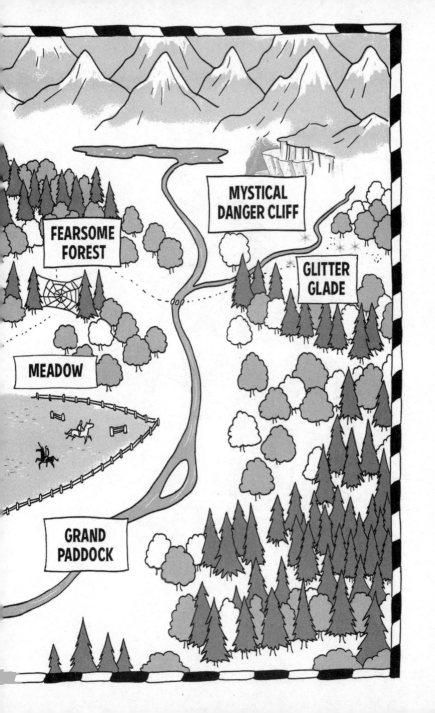

Contents

CHAPTER ONE
Magic Monday

It was Monday morning and Mira Desai was VERY excited. This was no ordinary Monday morning. This Monday morning was the first day of summer vacation AND it was Mira's first day at a new school! Because this was no ordinary school . . . this was:

UNICORN SCHOOL!

Mira had been desperate to go to Unicorn School since her sister, Rani, started going two summers ago. Rani wouldn't stop going on

about how wonderful her unicorn, Angelica, was. She kept saying how *amazing* she was at all the magical quests. And she was always making whinnying noises in Mira's ear to make her jealous. AND she'd brought home about a hundred Unicorn School quest medals, which had their own special shelf in the living room.

Rani said that quests could go on for days and days and were super exciting. And the time Rani spent at Unicorn School did seem *endless* to Mira. But time passed differently at Unicorn School, and Rani was really only ever gone for a day in normal time.

Mira had dreamed of having her own unicorn since FOREVER. She practiced braiding the manes and tails of all her toy horses, persuaded her dad to let her groom his beard, and even tried attaching a horn to their cat, Pickles. He wasn't very pleased.

3

It was a bit of a mystery who was selected to go to Unicorn School and who wasn't. Lots of people from Mira's family *had* gone to Unicorn School, including Mira's mom, so Mira had hoped more than anything that she would get to go, too. Mira always tried to live her life as open to magic as possible. She wished on stars, she believed in fairies, she said hello to black cats who crossed her path. And then, one incredible day, Mira had woken up with a sparkly envelope on her pillow.

Mira remembered it as if it were yesterday. (It was actually last Thursday.) She screamed so loudly that Pickles flung himself off Mira's bed into a pile of dirty clothes, and Mira's dad came running in to check what was wrong.

But there was nothing wrong. Everything was finally right. Her hands shaking with excitement, Mira opened the letter.

Dear Mira Desai,

We are delighted to invite you to join us at Unicorn School. You will be in Class RED.

Please use the Magic Portal to access the school. We look forward to seeing you soon.

Yours sincerely,
Madame Shetland

"DAD!" Mira yelled, and started jumping on the bed. "I'M GOING TO UNICORN SCHOOL!"

Terrified, Pickles jumped onto Mira's dad's face and wouldn't let go of his beard. "Mfmfmfmf!" he said cheerfully, and gave Mira a thumbs-up before leaving the room and walking into the wall.

Mira reached inside the envelope and pulled out a leaflet containing all the information about the school, including a map and the School Rules. Mira thought she might faint with delight. Unicorn School was going to be AMAZING!

For one thing, Mira couldn't WAIT to bring home her own medals. She'd already started making a space for them on the shelf (and had *accidentally* knocked a couple of Rani's medals into Pickles's bowl).

But the thing Mira was MOST excited about was getting to meet her unicorn.

Her sister said that the unicorns were *specially* chosen for each person for specific magical reasons. You would get to spend all day every day with your unicorn: going to lessons, working on projects, and going on quests. Basically your unicorn would be your best friend.

Mira had a best friend already at normal school (Katie with a *K*), but she could definitely squeeze another one into her life. She'd spent a lot of time thinking about her dream unicorn best friend (Princess Delilah Sparklehoof). She'd filled a whole notebook with drawings of her and made a list of all the incredible things they would do together.

UBFs 4 EVER

1. Have amazing, magical adventures!

2. Be great at quests

3. Get TONS OF MEDALS

Before heading to the Magic Portal that would take them to Unicorn School, Mira's mom took them to the supermarket. Mira and Rani needed

to get treats for their unicorns, and Mom needed
to buy doughnuts for someone's birthday at work.
Mira wondered what treats unicorns liked.

MAGIC BEANS

GLITTER CLOUDS

RAINBOW JUICE

MR. SPRINKLES!

Which aisle do you go to for magic treats?
she thought to herself. But when she asked her
sister, Rani rolled her eyes and said, "Unicorns
like carrots, *obviously.*" And so they all headed
over to the vegetable aisle.

When they'd bought their
carrots, they went back to the
car. Rani also had some hay
left over from last semester and Mom thought it
would be nice if she shared it with Mira.

The Magic Portal was in the parking lot by the
rec center. Mira had never actually seen it—the
portal could only be seen by current Unicorn
School students. Even Mira's mom couldn't see
it anymore, since she had left Unicorn School

roughly a thousand years ago. Usually when they dropped her off, Rani got out around the corner so that she wouldn't be seen with them. But TODAY Mira would be going with her. And she would be one step closer to meeting her unicorn!

There had been quite a bit of traffic on the way and Mom was running late for work.

"It's okay, Mom," said Rani. "I'll take Mira through."

Mom looked from one sister to the other and then at her watch.

"Fine," she said. And then she fixed Rani with a LOOK. "Make sure you take care of your little sister on her first day."

Mom handed them their treat bags, gave them

both a hug, and jumped back in the car. Rani had already started stomping off when Mom rolled down her window. She leaned out with her phone in hand.

"Girls! Let me take a picture. It's your first day at Unicorn School together!"

Rani turned, groaned, and folded her arms. "MOM, are you crying? That's so embarrassing."

Mom sniffed. "It brings back such amazing memories of MY first day at Unicorn School! Oh, happy times . . ." Their mom stared off into the distance for a moment, then she smiled and blew her nose. "Now, smile girls!"

Rani rolled her eyes. Mira smiled and gave two thumbs up as Mom's phone camera **CLICKED**.

"Love you, girls. Have fun!" Mom drove off,
waving one hand at them out of the window
as she left the parking lot. Mira felt a bit nervous.
"Where's the Magic Portal?" she asked Rani.
"Over here," her sister said. "Come on."

Rani stopped by the trash cans in the corner of the parking lot.

"So you have to get in the trash can, spin around three times, and then jump out and scream. Then you'll be at Unicorn School," she said.

Mira looked up at the trash can.

"Are you sure?" she said.

"Um, which one of us has a medal for being the Best at the Magic Portal?" said her sister.

"Okay . . . ," said Mira.

Mira climbed into the trash can and held her breath. This was SO exciting! (Also, it really stank.) In just a few seconds she'd be in Unicorn School . . .

UNICORN SCHOOL THIS WAY

CHAPTER TWO
Through the Portal

Mira leaped out of the trash can, yelling at the top of her lungs.

"AAAARRRRRRGGGGGGH!" came the reply, as she collided with someone.

Mira looked down to see a boy on the ground, staring up at her with wide eyes. Behind him was a man cowering by a bike rack.

"Oh, hello!" said Mira, as she helped the boy up. "Sorry about that."

The boy stared at her warily.

"So this is Unicorn School," she said, looking around.

To be honest, it didn't look very different from the rec center parking lot.

"Uh—no," said the man by the bike racks. Mira figured he must be the boy's dad because they looked quite alike and had matching briefcases. "This is where you go through the Magic Portal to get to the school. Raheem is just about to go through." He gestured at the boy, who gulped.

"But . . . ," said Mira, as she looked around for her sister, who was nowhere to be seen.

And then she realized—Rani had tricked her and gone through on her own! TYPICAL.

"We can show you if you like?" said Raheem's dad. "It's Raheem's first day. We've had twelve practice runs, just to be safe." He squeezed Raheem's shoulder.

"Do . . . do you live in that trash can?" squeaked Raheem.

"No! I was just . . . resting there before I went through the portal," said Mira. "It's my first day, too. I'm Mira. It would be great if you could show me."

She followed the two of them past the trash cans to a little clump of bushes at the edge of the parking lot.

19

Raheem and his dad showed her a gap in the branches where the air looked kind of wobbly and shimmery. *Magic*, thought Mira. Her tummy gave a little lurch. This was really it!

Mira waited for Raheem to say bye to his dad. It took a while because they checked Raheem's briefcase twice and then sang a song about the ten Rules of Keeping Safe. But finally, Mira and Raheem crawled through the gap in the bushes and into a clearing. Everything looked just a little bit sparkly.

"Okay," breathed Mira. "Ready?"

"Erfg," said Raheem.

Mira decided to take that as a yes. She grabbed

his arm with one hand and reached out toward the sparkles . . .

There was a flash of light that split into the seven colors of the rainbow. Mira felt herself

being lifted up, and before she knew it they were hurtling through the air.

Mira's toes tingled and a giggly feeling tickled up her legs, into her belly and arms and head. Even her hair felt excited. Everything was already so magical, she could hardly stand it. She was on her way to Unicorn School!

"HOW FUN IS THIS?" Mira yelled to Raheem, but he was too busy screaming to reply.

Just as quickly as it had appeared, the rainbow light vanished, and for a moment the two of them hung in the air, before dropping with a thump onto a soft haystack.

They climbed off the Landing Haystack just as more children were deposited by the rainbow.

Mira looked around and pulled strands of hay out of her hair. In front of them was Unicorn School. It was HUGE. It had turrets and a clock tower and looked a bit like a castle, but most of it was all on one level, like a bungalow. (*Because unicorns don't like stairs*, Mira remembered. There was nothing about unicorns that she didn't know.) Rani had told Mira that the dormitories, where the students slept at night, were up in the turrets, and the unicorns slept in their stables.

The stables were in a large cobbled yard in front of the school. On the other side of the yard were fields with jumps set up. *Those must be where the riding lessons are*, Mira thought. She had never been horse riding, but she had ridden a one-eared donkey at the beach last summer. She thought that unicorn riding *must* be easier than that—and there would be less chance of falling in the sea.

Behind the school, Mira could see the forest and, behind that, enormous ice-capped mountains. Rani said that the Fearsome Forest

was where lots of the quests took place. It was huge, stretching as far as Mira could see.

Mira's toes were still tingling. She turned to Raheem and grinned. He looked a little vomity from the journey.

The rainbow had dropped them off to the side of the Grand Paddock, which seemed to be the school playground for humans and unicorns. Real. Live. Actual. Unicorns! Groups of older kids stood chatting, each with a unicorn next to them, like it was no big deal. Mira realized her mouth was open in astonishment, and quickly closed it.

One group was playing soccer, but the players were *riding* their unicorns, and the unicorns were kicking the ball with their hooves! And over in a far corner of the field, some unicorns and their riders were leaping over the jumps. Mira thought they looked a little like they were flying. Rani had told her that the unicorns

developed magical powers as they got older,
and that some of them could fly!

The excited feeling in Mira's chest got bigger
and bigger until she felt like she might burst.
The unicorns were all amazing—different
colors, with long legs; sleek, glossy manes; and
glittery horns. It was amazing to think that
soon Mira would meet her very own unicorn!

Just then Mira heard a burst of laughter to her
right. There was Rani and her friends. They
were in their third year now—Class Yellow.
You started in Class Red and then moved up
through the colors of the rainbow. And each
year you had another stripe added to your
school badge. Mira looked at the badge on the

sleeve of her shirt. What would it look like when she had a full rainbow?

"Um," said Raheem, taking her out of her daydream. "I think we go over there."

Turning away from her sister, Mira followed Raheem to a big banner near the stables that read:

WELCOME TO UNICORN SCHOOL, CLASS RED!

CHAPTER THREE
Unicorn Best Friend Forever!

The bell in the clock tower chimed and everyone gathered in their classes. Mira's class was the only one with just humans—each of the other six class groups were made up of children *and* unicorns!

Seven teachers filed out of the school. Each of them wore a different-colored ribbon with their name on it. A tall, dark-haired teacher stopped in front of Mira's class. She was wearing a red ribbon that said, MISS GLITTERHORN.

"Good morning, Class Red," said Miss Glitterhorn.

"Good moooooorning, Miss Glitterhorn!" chorused Class Red.

"Now, before we head into assembly to meet the unicorns, I thought that it would be nice if we all got to know one another!" trilled Miss Glitterhorn.

Mira sighed. She was SO impatient to meet her new unicorn best friend . . . but she did like the idea of learning her classmates' names. After all, they would be her friends, too!

A girl at the front put her hand up. She had blond curly hair and was in a wheelchair with rainbow wheels.

"Yes?" Miss Glitterhorn beamed.

"Do you actually have a horn?"

30

"No, I don't," said Miss Glitterhorn. She smiled. "Now, we'll all play a getting-to-know-you game where—" The girl put her hand up again. "Yes?" said Miss Glitterhorn.

"Do you have unicorns in your family?"

"No, I don't," said Miss Glitterhorn. She smiled again, although it was a bit smaller this time. "So we—"

The girl put her hand up again. "So is it a coincidence that you are called Miss Glitterhorn?"

"YES," said Miss Glitterhorn. "Anyway—"

After seventeen questions, Miss Glitterhorn decided that actually they would go straight to the assembly and they could get to know one another on the way.

Mira and Raheem walked alongside the girl who'd been asking all the questions. She told them her name was Darcy and that she was going to be famous one day.

"Wow," said Raheem. "How will you be famous?"

Darcy shrugged. "I'll win a TV talent show probably."

"My dad says those shows are for people with

32

no talent," said a boy walking next to them. His footsteps were really loud and Mira saw that he was wearing cowboy boots. He had a mop of dirty-blond hair and a smug mouth. Mira had heard him saying earlier how his parents were Olympic show jumpers and were making sure he was given the best unicorn.

Darcy opened her mouth to reply, but they'd reached the hall and a stern-looking teacher gave her a warning look.

Mira gasped when she saw the Great Hall, which was in the center of the main school building. It was a beautiful indoor paddock, and the grass was sprinkled with wildflowers. At one end was a platform, with a glittery mounting

block next to it. Around the sides of the hall was a gallery for people to sit in. The other six classes were already there with their unicorns. Miss Glitterhorn pointed Class Red to the front row. Mira felt a flutter of pride. Her sister would be there to see her get her unicorn!

A hush descended on the hall, and a tiny woman walked across the paddock and onto the platform. Miss Glitterhorn joined her a moment later, clutching an armful of scrolls and a clipboard. The first woman introduced herself— she was Madame Shetland, the principal.

Madame Shetland cleared her throat and spoke into her microphone.

"Good morning, children and unicorns, and welcome to a new term at Unicorn School. And an extra special welcome to our new students, Class Red, who I trust have been busy learning the School Rules in preparation," said the principal. "Unicorn School is a place of fun, magic, and adventure—but it is something to be taken seriously. The bond between child and unicorn is a noble tradition, going back many centuries. Alongside your unicorn you will learn and grow. You will undertake quests and become the protectors of our land, and shine a glittery light throughout the unicorn world."

Mira felt a warm glow as she thought about how she would definitely take it seriously. And she would definitely follow ALL the rules. As soon as she knew what they were.

The principal smiled at the gathered students. "And, of course, even when not at Unicorn School you will take forth the lessons learned here and promote the principles of friendship, kindness, bravery, and tolerance."

After everyone applauded Madame Shetland, it was FINALLY time for the pairing of Class Red with their unicorns. Mira thought she might explode!

Miss Glitterhorn handed the principal the clipboard.

"Jake de Quincy," said Madame Shetland, looking at the clipboard.

Mira saw a boy walk up to the platform. He was the one with blond hair who was wearing cowboy boots. He was carrying his own riding helmet with golden wings over the ears.

Madame Shetland held the microphone toward Jake. "If you could tell us about yourself. Keep it brief."

Jake leaned in to the microphone. "I'm Jake. And I'm going to be a champion unicorn show jumper, just like my mom and dad."

Miss Glitterhorn handed Jake a scroll, which he held up in front of him.

"The name of your unicorn will appear on the scroll," declared Madame Shetland.

The class gasped as a projection of the scroll appeared on the wall behind him.

Jake

and

***

There was a hushed silence as they waited.
The scroll shimmered and then a blurry word
appeared. Everyone leaned forward to read it as
the letters gradually became clear and sharp.

Jake
and
Pegasus

Then there was a loud noise from the front of
the hall as the double doors swung open, making
them all jump. Mira let out an excited squeal and
Raheem nearly fell off his chair. Standing proudly
in the doorway was a sparkling, majestic unicorn.

He was deep purple with a dark blue mane and
a glittering golden horn. He strode toward the
mounting block where Jake waited with his helmet
in his hands and his eyebrows arched confidently.

Mira couldn't contain her excitement and gripped the hands of Raheem and Darcy, until Darcy muttered to her to "get off" and Raheem looked really uncomfortable.

Jake and Pegasus walked away from the platform to the other end of the hall, and Mira felt slightly relieved that they wouldn't have to ride the unicorns in front of everyone.

Darcy was the next to be called. She wheeled up a ramp and onto the platform. Madame Shetland held the microphone toward her and Darcy grabbed it.

"Wow. What can I say? This moment means SO much. I want to thank my mom—"

"A speech is not necessary, Darcy!" interrupted Madame Shetland.

Darcy's scroll appeared on the projection.

A dramatic whinny came from the double doors and the class turned to look. A unicorn came strutting in; her silver coat shimmered and caught the light as she walked. She arrived next to Darcy, swished her mane, and struck a pose. Darcy applauded in delight. They made their way over to Jake and Pegasus and started taking selfies until a teacher confiscated Darcy's phone.

Next was Seb, who said he loved art. He looked super excited to meet his unicorn, Firework, who had a rainbow-colored mane.

Then it was Raheem's turn. He stayed frozen to his seat when his name was called, so Mira gave

him an encouraging shove to get him to his feet.

"Good luck!" she whispered. He gulped and made

his way to the platform.

"My name is Raheem and I like books," he said

carefully into the microphone.

Raheem

and

***

I bet he gets a really clever unicorn, thought

Mira. *It'll probably be able to read and everything.*

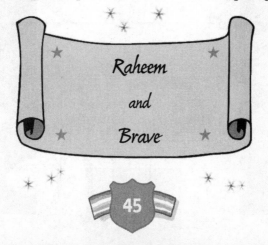

Raheem

and

Brave

A loud thundering sound could be heard from outside the hall and the floor seemed to shake. And then a blue shape came galloping into the hall. The unicorn was a blur, racing around the hall before coming to a sudden stop in front of the platform with a stamp of his front hoof. He was midnight blue and the biggest, tallest unicorn they'd seen so far.

Madame Shetland turned to Raheem, only to find he wasn't there. But she soon coaxed him out from behind the mounting block. Brave strutted over to the line of unicorns with Raheem following at a careful distance.

More and more children were called up. As each name was read out, Mira felt her heart leap into her throat and then sink back down again. Finally she looked around and realized she was the only one in Class Red without a unicorn.

"And finally we have Mira Des—" began Madame Shetland, and then she jumped when she saw Mira already standing next to her.

"I'm Mira. And I can't wait to meet my unicorn best friend," said Mira into the microphone.

She looked over at her sister in the crowd, who gave a deliberate yawn. "And I can't wait to win TONS of medals," said Mira. Madame Shetland looked at her and raised one eyebrow.

Miss Glitterhorn handed her the scroll. Mira's heart was hammering in her chest.

Mira

and

* * *

Everyone in the crowd turned toward the double doors. But there was no sign of her unicorn yet. Mira looked back down at her scroll.

She could see the word beginning to form.

It wasn't long enough to be Princess Delilah

Sparklehoof, but the first letter was a *D* . . .

Dancer? Dasher? DESTINY?

Mira

and

Dave

A surprised gasp echoed around the hall. Mira

peered closer at the scroll. It definitely said Dave.

Again the heads turned toward the door . . .

Again there was no unicorn.

Madame Shetland looked over at Miss

Glitterhorn, who said, "Just a sec," and jogged over

to the double doors. She started clicking and waving at something outside. But whatever was being clicked and waved at didn't seem to want to come in. Eventually Madame Shetland went over to help, and between them they pushed in the smallest, plumpest unicorn Mira had ever seen. He had his butt planted firmly on the ground and was making it as difficult as possible for the two teachers to move him.

Mira stared. He had a little potbelly and a mane like straw that stuck up at odd angles.

"Greet your unicorn, dear," said Madame Shetland, giving a slightly forced smile. Miss Glitterhorn was leaning against the mounting block and sweating.

"Hi . . . Dave," said Mira. The unicorn looked up at her. Okay, so he was a bit small. And he wasn't very glittery. *But at least I have a unicorn!* she thought.

Mira reached out to pat his nose, and Dave snorted loudly and put his ears back. She pulled her hand away.

"A round of applause for our final pair, Mira and Dave!" said Madame Shetland.

Uncertain claps rippled around the hall. Mira's sister was laughing so hard she had to be taken outside.

Mira looked back at her unicorn. There was a twinkle in Dave's eye. Mira felt encouraged. She smiled and waved at the crowd.

Dave snorted again and lifted his tail. Then he unleashed a giant heap of poop onto Miss Glitterhorn's feet.

CHAPTER FOUR
Dave's Doughnuts

It took Mira a while to get from assembly to her first lesson, as Dave had sat down again in the corridor and was refusing to move. But Raheem came to help her and together they half dragged, half pushed Dave down the hallway on his bottom and toward the classroom.

Unicorn School was certainly full of surprises. And challenges. Right now Dave was being quite a challenge, but Mira was sure they would have a magical time as soon as they got to class.

Miss Glitterhorn tutted when they finally

arrived. She was standing in front of the whiteboard, cleaning Dave's poop off her shoes with a wet wipe.

"As I was saying, Class Red, Unicorn School Rule 19 is Be on Time, Every Time."

Mira gasped. The double desks were like normal desks on one side, but on the other there was a taller, unicorn-sized desk with a bag of hay hanging off it. Underneath each unicorn's desk was a basket containing grooming equipment. Raheem scurried over to sit at the desk right at the front where Brave was standing proudly. There was one empty double desk. Dave plodded toward it, behind Mira, and gave a snort. Then he finished off his entire bag of hay in two bites.

They'd made it! Mira gave a happy sigh as she sat down at her desk.

Miss Glitterhorn finished running through the

School Rules (Mira definitely heard at least some of them) and stood up from behind her desk. "Now that you have your unicorns," she said, "the lessons can begin. We will have three days of lessons, where you will learn all about Unicorn School and how we look after the land. But, most important, you will bond with your unicorns so that on day four, you will be ready to go on your first magical quest."

The class oohed and aahed, and there was a buzz of excitement. Mira looked around the room and noticed that Jake and Pegasus were their neighbors. She gave Jake a friendly smile, but he was looking at Dave with a disgusted expression on his face. She turned and saw that Dave was gnawing at the corner of the desk. She hoped Miss Glitterhorn wouldn't notice.

"Right!" said Miss Glitterhorn. "Lesson one is Getting to Know Your Unicorn. You and your unicorn have a *very* special bond. You were chosen for each other by the purest kind of magic: friendship. But you've only just met and you must earn your unicorn's trust. First, grooming. This is very relaxing for unicorns. Pick up your brushes and off you go!"

Mira picked up a soft brush. She'd read all about grooming. She reached out to put the brush on Dave's back and he ducked, avoiding her hand, and sidestepped out of the way.

Mira stepped closer to him and tried again, but he just did the same thing. Then she tried a different brush, but he sidestepped again. They kept doing this and shuffling farther and farther away from their desk until a girl named Tamsin put her hand up to say that they were making her unicorn feel uncomfortable.

Mira dragged Dave back to their desk. She tried hiding the brush behind her back. She tried attaching it to a stick. She even tried brushing herself to show him how nice it was, until

 Miss Glitterhorn came over to ask what she was doing. Then, hoping to put him in a better mood, Mira gave Dave the unicorn crown

she'd made for him. Dave looked at the crown thoughtfully for a moment and then he ate it.

Mira suddenly had a brilliant idea. Dave must be hungry! That's why he wasn't paying attention!

Mira remembered Miss Glitterhorn saying Treating Is Cheating (Unicorn School Rule 54) and You Must Not Bribe Your Unicorn (Unicorn School Rule 3), but this was tending to Dave's needs. She was looking after him! She reached into her bag for the treats she'd bought with Mom earlier.

But the shopping bag was full of doughnuts, not carrots! Mira realized she must have picked up her mom's bag by mistake . . . Now Dave didn't have ANY treats. (And Mom had taken a bag of carrots to work with her.) Mira could feel her eyes welling up with tears as she dropped the doughnuts on the floor. NOTHING was going right today.

But something extraordinary was happening to Dave. His nostrils flared and his mouth twitched. With a happy little whinny he gobbled up a doughnut, then another, and before Mira could stop him he had eaten them all AND the bag.

Suddenly, Dave was like a different unicorn. His eyes shone and his mane even looked swishy. He let Mira stroke his soft muzzle and then he stamped a hoof in joy. Mira grabbed a brush and started combing it through his mane. She looked around the room, fizzing with pride. She hoped everyone would see how happy Dave suddenly was—he was showing his teeth in a sort of weird grin. *He must really like doughnuts*, she thought. Maybe she would win a medal for Best at Cheering Up Unicorns!

Then it all went wrong.

Dave reared up on his hind legs and let out a loud and gleeful neigh. He shot forward, knocking over a chair. A few children and unicorns turned toward them, startled, and Miss Glitterhorn looked up from her desk.

Then, full of sugary, doughnutty joy,

Dave galloped around the classroom, scattering the students and their unicorns and destroying the matchstick fairy-tale castle that Grace Hobbs had brought in as a present for her unicorn and had taken "literally weeks to make." Finally he skidded into Jake's desk and crushed his pencil case. Jake looked furious.

After Miss Glitterhorn had wrangled Dave into

the Naughty Stall, she announced that since *most* students had successfully groomed their unicorns, the class would now be creating pieces of art together. She suggested that Mira use the time to read the rule book, paying special attention to Unicorn School Rule 79: No Havoc Indoors.

"That's one Havoc Point already, I'm afraid. Three Havoc Points will result in detention," she said. "Then, that student and their unicorn will not be able to attend the first quest."

Mira felt a panicky feeling in her stomach. She couldn't miss out on the first quest!

She snuck a look at Dave over her shoulder and saw that he was happily snoozing in the Naughty Stall. He looked very sweet. But she couldn't quite ignore the thought she kept pushing to the back of her mind.

What if they didn't have a totally magical bond? What if Dave *wasn't* going to be her unicorn best friend?

CHAPTER FIVE
History Comes Alive ...

After a good night's sleep in Red Dormitory, Mira woke up feeling full of hope for the day ahead. She picked Dave up from his stable and gave him a little pep talk on the way to class. At least he was walking alongside her today. Mira felt that was progress.

"I know it feels different being in school now, like a big unicorn. But we'll get through it together! I know we can be best friends!"

Dave gave Mira a sideways glance and then let out a long, rumbling fart.

The first lesson of the day was History of the Unicorn, and their teacher, Mr. Trotsky, was giving a lecture on famous unicorns of the last thousand years. Mira lost concentration a couple of times, first when another class rode their unicorns past the window and then when Darcy passed around a note saying, "Would you rather have a unicorn that could breathe fire or one that had electric hooves?" And Mr. Trotsky did have a slow, droney voice.

"I hope you've been taking notes, class," Mr. Trotsky said, after talking for a very long time. "We have another five hundred years of unicorns to get through after our break, and then you will each prepare a presentation about a famous unicorn from history, to be performed at the end of the day. Let's make history come alive!"

After break time, Dave trotted over to the grooming basket under their desk. With his front hoof, he knocked everything out of the basket, lay down in it, and went to sleep.

Mira looked around at the other unicorns who were sitting up nicely at their desks. Some were even helping to take notes. Seb's unicorn, Firework, seemed to be sketching with his horn.

I'm sure Dave can do that, too . . . when he's awake, thought Mira. She smiled and picked out different colored pens to underline her notes. That cheered her up.

Top Five Best Unicorns from History

- <u>Unicornardo da Vinci</u> — painter and inventor
- King Henry the Neighth — <u>very fat unicorn</u> who had six wives
- Abraham Linc-horn — maybe the <u>greatest</u> unicorn president
- Queen Boudiccorn — the <u>most magnificent</u> Celtic warrior queen unicorn
- King Arth-horn and the Unicorns of the Round Stable

"Hey," hissed Jake from beside her. "Don't you know Unicorn School Rule 23?"

Mira shook her head.

Jake rolled his eyes. "Unicorns Must Be Awake During Lessons," he said. Pegasus widened his eyes, as if to demonstrate what being awake was.

Mira looked down at Dave, who was snoring. She nudged him with her foot and Dave let out

a giant fart. Freya's unicorn, Princess, bolted out of the classroom in fright.

Mr. Trotsky went to retrieve Princess, and Mira felt a tap on her shoulder. It was Freya.

"Sorry I scared your unicorn away," said Mira.

"Oh, don't worry," said Freya. "She's scared of everything. It's nice to have a break."

"Well, at least your unicorn's awake," said Mira.

"She's TOO awake!" Freya laughed. "Here," she said, handing Mira her sunglasses. "Put these on him and then Mr. Trotsky will never notice."

They carefully put the sunglasses on Dave's head. Now you couldn't tell he was asleep! Then, just to be sure, Freya got out her silver pen and drew eyes on the lenses.

Mr. Trotsky returned with Princess. He
glanced briefly at Dave before heading back to
his desk. Mira breathed in relief. They'd gotten
away with it!

When it was time to do their presentations,
Dave was STILL asleep. Luckily, Darcy
volunteered to go first. Darcy and her unicorn

performed a rap ("Darcy and Star, the best by far") and a complicated interpretive dance based on Darcy's favorite Disney film. Mr. Trotsky said they did very well to keep going for such a long time, but he couldn't give them credit because it had nothing to do with history.

Eventually it was time for Mira and Dave. Dave was still asleep and was now gnashing his teeth loudly. (Mira thought he might be sleep eating.) With some help from Raheem and Freya, Mira dragged Dave's basket to the front. Old Mr. Trotsky peered at him suspiciously.

"I am here to tell you the story of a unicorn who has, until now, remained hidden in history!" declared Mira. She pointed at Dave. "The Great

Dave-ius III. He was really good friends with Cleopatra and Marco Polo." Mira looked at Mr. Trotsky, who was frowning. "One day the Great Dave-ius III really annoyed a witch and she turned him to STONE!"

The class gasped.

Mira pointed at Dave again. "He was frozen. He could not do anything except stare with his beautiful silver eyes. He was a statue for a hundred years."

"What happened then?" piped up Flo, Freya's twin sister, from the front row.

"Um . . . ," said Mira. The class looked expectantly at Dave. Who did nothing.

"And then he died. The end!" said Mira.

There was silence. Flo started clapping, but then she stopped.

Mira took a bow, but as she swept down, she knocked the sunglasses and they tumbled off Dave's head and onto the floor.

"His EYES fell off!" shrieked Flo, and she fainted.

"YOUR UNICORN IS ASLEEP!" bellowed Mr. Trotsky, as Flo's unicorn, Sparkles, prodded her with a hoof. "That," said Mr. Trotsky, "is a Havoc Point."

ONE
HAVOC POINT

ONE
HAVOC POINT

CHAPTER SIX
Perfect Prancing

"Maybe Dave's just tired after the lesson?" said Raheem at lunch, as they ate their Rainbow Pie. (Rainbow Pie had seven different-colored vegetables in it. Mira didn't think that was very magical.)

They all looked at Dave. After finishing his lunch in about three seconds, he'd gone back to sleep.

"Maybe he just doesn't like you?" said Darcy.

"What?!" Mira spat out her Rainbow Pie.

Darcy shrugged. "Just saying. He's getting you in trouble a lot."

"We can swap if you like?" said Freya. She hadn't been able to eat yet because Princess was hugging her so hard she couldn't move her arms. Raheem looked up. He was having a unicorn-free lunch. Brave had gone outside to charge around and leap over jumps.

"You can't swap your unicorn!" said Darcy, shocked.

Mira was a little sad. She didn't really feel like she'd bonded with Dave yet. Mostly he'd been asleep, grumpy, or naughty. BUT he was who he was. And he was her unicorn!

Mira shook her head firmly. "No," she said. "Dave *does* like me. He'll get the hang of school soon."

"He'd better hurry up," a voice chimed in. They looked up to see Jake standing by their table looking smug. "If you want to go on the quest that is. You already have TWO Havoc Points and if you get three then that's detention and you have to stay here while we all go questing."

"I wouldn't mind getting detention and staying here," muttered Raheem, as Jake and Pegasus strode away. Mira crossed her arms. There was NO WAY she was getting another Havoc Point and missing the quest!

Mira and Dave managed to keep out of trouble for the rest of the day. And the next morning it was time for their first riding lesson!

Miss Glitterhorn had said that the best rider would be given the honor of leading the quest. Jake had told them all that he'd been taking riding lessons since he was a baby, so he was 100 percent sure he was going to be quest leader. Mira knew she wouldn't be the best, but she didn't care about being particularly good at riding—just as long as she and Dave made it on to the quest.

Class Red filed into the meadow at the front of the school. It was being decorated for the first quest party. Glittery flags hung from trees and hedges. Class Green was blowing up balloons and Class Indigo was helping Miss Ponytail, the art teacher, set up a giant knitted scene of the Great Quest of 1488 (that was when Unicornardo da Vinci invented a horned helicopter and flew it over Diamond Lake).

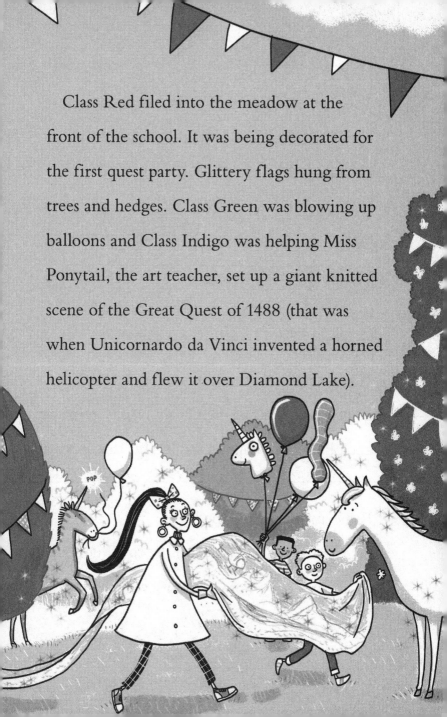

The first quest was a BIG deal at Unicorn School. When Class Red had completed their quest, the entire school would come out to celebrate with them.

"What do you think the quest will be?" Flo said, hopping from foot to foot with excitement. She was wearing a homemade horn that wobbled back and forth.

"I bet we'll have to climb a mountain and then probably fight a witch," said Darcy, pointing at the glittery ice-capped mountains that loomed behind the forest.

Raheem looked alarmed.

Jake smirked. "My dad said the first quest is always super dangerous and not everyone makes it back—only the BEST unicorns and their riders."

Raheem had to go sit down.

Miss Glitterhorn rounded up Class Red by clapping her hands. "It's time for your riding lesson, class! Please escort your unicorns to the stables to glitter-shoe their hooves."

"Miss, Miss!" Darcy waved her hand in the air. "What are glitter shoes?"

"Don't you know ANYTHING?" Jake scoffed. "They're not glitter shoes, it's 'glitter-shoe.' Unicorns need glitter to protect their hooves before they can be ridden. There's a glitter-shoe box outside every stall."

"Thank you, Jake, but be nice, please," said

81

Miss Glitterhorn. "Yes, glitter is *very* important for unicorns. It keeps their hooves safe and makes their horns sparkle. But the horn glitter is only for *very* special occasions. Now, hurry up, everyone. Glitter-shoe your friends!"

Once the unicorns all had glittered feet (and Darcy had glitter-rimmed her wheels), they lined up in the paddock. Miss Glitterhorn showed them how to mount a unicorn using the mounting block. Darcy had an awesome harness that helped her out of her chair and onto Star. Raheem thought it looked like a much safer way to get on Brave, but Miss Glitterhorn wouldn't let him use it.

Dave stood very calmly next to the mounting block while Mira put her helmet on. That was a good start, she thought. But then she tried getting

onto him, and Dave kicked up his back legs

and tipped her into a bush.

Mira picked a clump of leaves out of her hair.

She stroked Dave's muzzle and gently placed both

hands on his back and climbed onto . . . nothing

as Dave trotted to the other side of the fence.
Mira landed with a thump on the grass.

This. Was. Not. Fair!

The others were happily mounting and
dismounting their unicorns and practicing going
from a walk to a trot around the edges of the
paddock.

Mira could feel tears pricking at her eyes.
Why didn't Dave let her ride? Why wouldn't
he behave properly? WHY was he making
Unicorn School so difficult? All Mira had ever
wanted was to come here and make a unicorn
best friend and earn tons of medals so she could
put them on the shelf at home. Was that TOO
MUCH TO ASK?

Mira was really crying now. She put her hands over her face so that no one could see. She felt a nudge at her back.

Looking over her shoulder, she saw Dave. Mira sniffed. "Leave me alone, Dave."

But Dave ducked down and, with a flick of his nose, tipped Mira up and onto his back. Then he trotted over to the rest of the class and joined the back of the line, as the unicorns took turns weaving in and out of sparkly cones set up all around the field.

Mira sniffed loudly and wiped her nose on the sleeve of her shirt. Then she leaned down to give Dave a hug. "Thank you," she whispered.

Dave flicked his ears in response.

Over the next couple of hours, they practiced walking, trotting, and cantering, plus communicating with their unicorns using their voices and their bodies. Dave didn't put a hoof wrong—and Mira couldn't stop grinning!

Then it was time to learn the unicorn and rider's most important skill: prancing. The unicorns had to pick their feet up high and bounce along. It was a bit like trotting and very bumpy. Miss Glitterhorn shouted words of encouragement. "Good, Jake, but straighten your back. Not so bouncy, Flo! Raheem, just GET BACK on your unicorn . . . Excellent. Who's that? Mira! Mira?! Oh! Gosh! Well— excellent, well done. Lovely prancing!"

Mira was so surprised at getting praise from Miss Glitterhorn that she nearly fell off Dave!

Darcy grinned and held up her hand for a high five when Mira got back to the line. "You guys are totally going to get a Best at Prancing medal!"

Mira couldn't quite believe it. For the first time, lessons were going well at Unicorn School. She stroked Dave's scratchy mane between his ears. He gave a proud fart.

Miss Glitterhorn clapped to get their attention again. "I'm delighted to say that, for the loveliest prancing I've seen in a long time, our leaders for the first quest will be . . . Mira and Dave!"

Mira thought she might actually burst with pride.

"But . . . ," Jake blurted out.

"Yes, Jake?" said Miss Glitterhorn, looking surprised.

"But my dad was quest leader on all the quests he ever did. He . . ." Jake's voice wavered, and

he looked down and twiddled his fingers. Mira thought he might be crying.

"Oh, Jake," said Miss Glitterhorn, "there will be plenty of chances to be the leader. Now, one more prance around the paddock, then it's dinnertime!"

The unicorns got into line, but Jake was still looking down and fiddling with something in his pocket. Mira nudged Dave with her foot and they rode over to Jake and Pegasus.

"Are you okay?" said Mira. And then she stopped. "Is that a doughnut? Why do you have . . . ?"

With a sly grin, Jake threw the doughnut across the paddock. Dave bolted after the snack, which sailed over the fence.

Mira clung desperately onto Dave's mane. Everything around her was a blur! Dave soared over the fence and thudded down on the other side.

Mira could see people and unicorns scattering and objects flying in all directions. Something was ahead of them . . . A colorful, glittering rectangular shape stretched across their path.

Then suddenly, Dave skidded to a halt—Mira lurched forward, but she clung on. She saw the doughnut lying on the ground just in front of them.

"Phew!" she panted, sitting up straight. Then Dave gave a buck and Mira was tipped off his back. She went straight through the glittery shape and landed with a bump on the grass. She could hear voices saying strange things like "The mural!" and "I spent five years knitting that!"

"That—Mira Desai—is a Havoc Point," said a very angry Miss Glitterhorn.

Mira stood up dizzily. "But, wait . . . No! Three Havoc Points means . . ."

Miss Glitterhorn frowned. "No quest for you."

CHAPTER SEVEN
An Unexpected Quest

Mira sat in the classroom, looking at her drawing of Princess Delilah Sparklehoof. Everyone else had gone to the first quest farewell ceremony. She could hear them all cheering outside. Mira didn't want to go to the ceremony. She knew she'd feel even worse watching the rest of the class going off on their quest and seeing how excited they all were.

Jake had denied all knowledge of the doughnut and was made quest leader. The mural that Mira had sailed straight through, making a big hole, was currently being repaired by Class Yellow.

Mira sighed and put the Princess Delilah Sparklehoof picture in her bag. Then she set off for the PE office, where she'd been told to go for her detention. As she walked down the corridor, she heard a snort and turned to see Dave trotting beside her. He nosed around in her bag.

"I don't have any snacks, Dave," said Mira. Dave pulled out the Princess Delilah Sparklehoof picture.

"NO! Don't eat that!" Mira snatched the picture back and smoothed it down. "Princess Delilah wouldn't have gotten me in trouble," she said quietly.

Dave looked at Mira and blinked. Then he continued trotting down the corridor.

When they reached the office, a fierce-looking PE teacher named Miss Hind was sitting behind a desk.

But she wasn't the only person in the room.

"Darcy!" exclaimed Mira. "What are you doing here? Shouldn't you be on the quest?"

"TELL me about it," cried Darcy. "It's an absolute outrage! I have been making a VITAL contribution in every lesson." Star snorted in support.

"Yes," said Miss Hind, "but you haven't done any of your work."

Just then, in walked Raheem and Brave.

"What are YOU doing here?" said Mira and Darcy together.

"I'm in detention," he said.

Darcy frowned. "*Really?* What did you do?"

"I put unicorn poop in Miss Glitterhorn's bag

and got three Havoc Points at once!" he replied, his eyes wide, almost as though he couldn't believe it himself.

"WHAT?!" said Darcy.

Unicorn poop was very small and neat and glittery, but it was still poop.

The teacher grunted from her desk and gestured for them to be quiet.

"Why would you get put in detention on purpose?" Mira whispered, as Raheem sat down.

"I thought you might like some company!" Raheem grinned.

Mira wondered if it was more about not having to go on the quest, but she didn't say anything.

Brave seemed quite angry with Raheem and was refusing to look at him.

"Did you hear what the task was?" asked Darcy.

"No," said Mira glumly.

"It's GLITTER PICKING," Darcy replied. "It sounds absolutely *awful*. I'm *glad* we're not going."

I'd happily go glitter picking, thought Mira, as the teacher told them to stop talking.

∪∪∪

Miss Hind led them into the stables. She pointed to a pile of dustpans and brooms and a poop shovel, and told them that their detention task would be mucking out ALL the unicorn stables. Then she turned and headed into the PE office. They heard her turn on the TV.

"What?" said Raheem, horrified. "I thought we'd be writing lines or tidying up the stationery cupboard!"

"More poop for you, Raheem!" Darcy giggled. "Well, have fun. Star and I have stuff to do." They scooted off to the other side of the stables, where they appeared to be looking at photos on Darcy's phone.

Mira wondered if you could get medals in detention. She hadn't imagined her first medal would be Best at Picking Up Poop, but at least it would BE a medal.

"Come on," she said. "We have a lot of poop to get through."

It wasn't so bad at first—the neat little unicorn

poops were pretty easy to pick up. But Dave's poops, of course, were different. They were sloppy and messy. And giant. Every time they cleared a stable, he would add a new poop on top of the straw, like it was a fun game.

Mira paused for a moment and stared out toward the forest. She wondered what Class Red was doing now.

Then she saw a bolt of glittery light shoot up from the trees and into the sky.

"Guys!" she shouted. "Quick!"

"What?" said Raheem nervously.

Darcy wheeled over. "Hey, how's it going? Oh, Raheem, you missed a bit."

"They set off a flare!" said Mira. "I read about flares in the handbook." She tried hard to remember what it had said. She had been distracted by the photos of the unicorns . . .

Then she remembered something Rani had told her. "OH! It could be a DISTRESS FLARE! It's a signal that means they're in danger!"

Raheem's eyes went wide, but Darcy looked unsure. "They're *glitter picking*," she said. "The worst that could happen is someone could get trapped in a trash bag."

"Actually, they collect the glitter in special boxes," said Raheem. "And it's really valuable. And they said at the farewell ceremony that they need to collect tons to fill the Great Horn at the quest party, and they collect it at the Glitter Glade, which is an amazingly special place. So glitter picking is a *really* important que— Ow!"

Darcy elbowed him and looked pointedly at Mira. "It's a *silly* quest and we are *not* missing out."

Mira looked out one more time, but the forest was still and silent. She sighed. The Glitter Glade sounded completely magical. She wished she were there now.

A few minutes later something made them all stop. A long, low howl rang out from the forest.

HhhhooOO**wwwwllllll**

It got louder and louder, and then was accompanied by other sounds—screeches and rumbles. They all looked at one another.

"The Dangers of the Forest," whispered Raheem fearfully.

"What?" Mira frowned.

"I read a book before I came here about all the possible dangers that lurk within the Fearsome Forest," Raheem said. "There were ninety-seven. And lots of them can be identified by their sound. That could have been a bear, or a werewolf, or an earthquake—an avalanche . . ."

More howling and moaning rang out from the forest.

LLL HHHhhooOOO WwwwLLLLLLLLL

Hhhhhoooo00 WwwwLLLLL

hooOO HHHhhooOOOW

"A land whale?" suggested Darcy.

"Should we go and get Miss Hind?" said Mira. She felt weirdly excited. Obviously she didn't want Class Red to be in danger, but if they were, they would need rescuing . . .

"She might think we're being silly," said Raheem.

Miss Hind *did* think they were being silly. She said the forest made all sorts of noises and that they'd probably imagined the flare. And she was very annoyed that they had interrupted her during a crucial moment in Champion WUWF (Worldwide Unicorn Wrestling Federation).

"I'm *sure* something's wrong," said Mira, as they walked into the yard. "What if they

ARE in danger and we don't do anything at all? We can't just stay here and do nothing!"

She paused for a moment and stared at Dave and then back at the forest. "Team. I think it's time for a RESCUE QUEST!"

CHAPTER EIGHT
The Fearsome Forest

Darcy was very much up for the adventure, and Raheem reluctantly agreed that they should make sure everyone was okay, as long as he could take some essential items with him on the trip. The items that Raheem considered essential were: his *Dangers of the Forest* book, a first-aid kit, a flashlight, sunscreen, antibacterial ointment, two changes of clothes, a waterproof coat and pants, a reflective jacket, knee pads, a notebook, his special rock collection, his lucky teddy bear, three packed lunches, and an extra pair of emergency socks.

Brave was stamping his foot at the entrance
to the stable yard, impatient for them to get
going. He had stopped ignoring Raheem now
that they were going on a quest, and he was
only a little annoyed when he realized how
heavy Raheem's backpack was.

"RIGHT!" shouted Mira. "We are going. On a QUEST. And we are going to rescue our class and we are going to get a medal for it. And we are going to have THE TIME OF OUR LIVES!"

Mira rustled some treats until Dave woke up, and then she jumped on his back.

"Okay, people," said Darcy. "It's showtime. Which way are we going?"

Mira blinked hard and held out the map of the school grounds. Dave turned around and sniffed at it. "Class Red was heading to the Glitter Glade. So, we . . . we take that path and follow it into the forest, and then just as the path splits we—"

Dave ate the map.

MUuunCcchHHHH

Raheem sighed. "Well, now that we don't have the map, we'd better stay here."

"We don't need maps," said Darcy. "We'll follow our HEARTS! Or . . . just pick a random path and go for it."

Star set off on the bridle path out of the school grounds. Raheem squealed as Brave galloped after them.

Mira gave Dave a pat on the neck. He did one last poop, and then they set off after their friends.

Everything seemed so much more bright and shiny to Mira as they rode to the edge of the paddock. This was a quest! An ACTUAL quest!

The entrance to the forest was shrouded in sparkly cobwebs, and they began to pick their way carefully through them.

"Brave's stopped!" called Raheem, still outside the forest.

Mira turned Dave around. "It's okay, Raheem," she said. "It's not that dark and terrifying in here, I promise!"

It took a while but Raheem and Brave *finally* came trotting through. "It really was Brave, not me," said Raheem grumpily. "He wouldn't move."

As they made their way through the forest, there was less birdsong and they could only just glimpse the sky through the thick branches up above them. Even though it was a little spooky, Mira couldn't help but feel happy. She was on an actual QUEST (sort of), and Dave had been awake for hours!

"I wish we didn't have to trek through this terrifying forest," muttered Raheem. He was struggling to stay on Brave, who kept backing away from cobwebs and snorting wildly.

"I know what will distract us," said Darcy, moving Star away from Brave, who was shaking his mane. "Let's sing the school song!" She began to sing loudly and somewhat tunelessly:

"We love our unicorns, yes we do!

We keep them safe and glitter their shoes—"

Brave suddenly gave a strange, high-pitched whinny and Raheem pointed at the path ahead of them. It was blocked by three huge tree trunks.

"Oh no!" said Mira. "I'm sure we're getting close to Class Red now." She jumped off Dave and climbed up one of the tree trunks, brushing aside more of the sparkly cobwebs. "Yes! The path forks just up ahead, and the Glitter Glade should be down the hill on the left."

"Let's jump it," said Darcy, backing Star up to get ready.

Brave started shaking. "I think he's trying to tell us something," said Raheem.

"He probably just wants to go first," said Mira. "Brave by name, brave by nature!"

At that, Brave knelt down on the path and put his hooves over his eyes.

Raheem looked down at his unicorn and

then up at the tree trunks. "Maybe he's scared of heights?" Brave snorted indignantly and shook his head.

"Look, Brave, Star and I will go first," said Darcy. "You'll be fine!"

Star cantered up to the logs and jumped clean over them. Darcy let out a happy whoop on the other side.

Mira hopped back onto Dave and pointed him toward the trunks.

"What do you think, Dave?"

Dave ran straight at the trunks . . . and then scrambled through a gap at the bottom of the trees, scaring away spiders and cobwebs,

115

with Mira clinging on to his back. It was a clever way to get through, Mira had to admit, even though she'd swallowed a cobweb or two.

Moments later Raheem and Brave came soaring over the trunks.

"It was the spiders!" said Raheem. "As soon as Dave scared them away, Brave was fine!"

The unicorns and the children all high-fived one another, though Brave still looked a bit shaky.

"It's okay, boy." Raheem patted his unicorn's neck. "Spiders are harmless really. We got through it together!"

"Come on, Team Rescue Quest!" called Mira. She was still buzzing from getting past the tree trunks. NOTHING was going to stop them!

Well, until the unicorns' hooves slipped and
the friends found themselves tumbling down a
steep, muddy, leaf-covered hill . . .

CHAPTER NINE
To the Rescue!

Mira opened her eyes, rubbing her sore head. She was at the bottom of a pile of Raheem, Darcy, and their three unicorns, at the foot of the steep slope. Then a big shape loomed over them. It said, "YOU are supposed to be in detention."

"Miss Glitterhorn!" said Mira. "We found you! We're here to rescue you!"

Their teacher helped Mira and the others up. Mira could see that they were in the Glitter Glade! It was a beautiful grassy clearing in the trees, with streams of glitter running down

from the hills nearby. Everything sparkled. The
unicorns were holding ornate-looking boxes in
their teeth, which the students were filling with
glitter from the sparkly piles on the glade floor.

But, Mira realized, no one seemed to be in
any trouble. Everyone in Class Red looked . . .
well, fine. They were all staring at Mira and her
friends, mid–glitter scoop.

"Uh . . . we don't need rescuing?" said Jake, making a face at them.

"But . . . you sent up a glitter flare to ask for help." Mira was suddenly unsure of herself.

"A what?" Miss Glitterhorn crossed her arms. "Mira, that was a glitter *cannon* to celebrate the start of the quest."

"But . . . we heard a moaning and wailing sound. We thought something terrible was after you!" Darcy said, pulling leaves out of her hair.

Freya stepped forward and rolled her eyes. "That was lunchtime. The unicorns wanted to sing karaoke."

"That's enough, Freya, you know the unicorns love to sing." Miss Glitterhorn sighed.

As if on cue, Firework and Sparkles burst into a howl, and then Princess joined in with several bloodcurdling screams.

Mira winced. It sounded like the time she had accidentally sat on Pickles.

Miss Glitterhorn stared at Mira and her friends angrily. "You are all in BIG trouble. We will deal with this when we get back to the school."

Mira's heart was thumping. Could you get EXPELLED from Unicorn School?

Freya appeared at Mira's side. "Don't worry. The quest hasn't been that fun. You didn't miss much."

They looked over at Freya's sister, Flo, who

121

was rolling around in glitter with Sparkles and laughing with joy. Seb ran past with an armful of glitter, shouting, "THIS IS SO MUCH FUN!!"

"Well, it's a little bit fun," admitted Freya.

"But Jake's in a terrible mood because Miss Glitterhorn said we couldn't collect the rainbow glitter from the edge of the Mystical Danger Cliff. It's too dangerous for first years—you have to be Class Green or above."

"Very sensible," said Raheem.

Just then the glade darkened as clouds appeared in the sky.

Miss Glitterhorn clapped her hands and told the rest of the class to hurry up. "Almost time to return to school, children! Remember, we must collect enough glitter to fill the Great Horn so the unicorns can glitter their horns at the party. And there is an extra medal for whoever collects the most glitter!"

And then the rain started. It was the suddenest, heaviest rain shower Mira had ever seen. The children were all soaked through within seconds. Darcy and Star and Raheem and Brave sped over to the nearest tree for shelter.

Mira was about to follow when she heard a noise. She stopped, straining to listen over the rain. It sounded like someone calling for help . . .

Mira knew her teacher wouldn't believe her, not after the rescue quest turned out to be— well, neither a rescue *nor* a quest. And Miss Glitterhorn was busy gathering the class and the glitter together. Mira looked over at her friends sheltering under the tree. She couldn't risk getting them into even more trouble.

But what if she was right this time?

She looked around to check that no one was watching her, then gave Dave a nudge, and they both crept off down the path in the direction of the sound.

The path under their feet became rockier. Then they saw a sign that said, MYSTICAL DANGER CLIFF UP AHEAD. Then another one that said, CLASS GREEN AND ABOVE ONLY PAST THIS POINT. Mira and Dave looked at each other.

"Should we do it?" said Mira.

Dave trotted over to the sign and kicked it into a bush, and then looked back at Mira.

Well that was one way of dealing with it.

Then they saw it. An enormous cliff face covered in rainbow glitter. A narrow, rocky path led across the side of the cliff to the edge, which jutted out over a ravine. There had been some sort of landslide, and the path was blocked by a huge mound of glitter. Standing against the cliff edge, on the other side of the mound, were Jake and Pegasus.

"Jake? JAKE!"

"Mira?"

Jake took a step along the narrow path toward her. A few glittery rocks crumbled off into the ravine below.

"Stop!" yelled Mira. "Wait there, I'll go get Miss Glitterhorn."

"NO!" Jake backed up against the cliff. "I . . . I don't want to get into trouble."

Mira hesitated. Jake and Pegasus really were in danger on the cliff path, but she didn't want to get him in trouble with Miss Glitterhorn. And Mira was in enough trouble herself already . . . She made up her mind.

"Jake, we have to get back to school safely.
Just stay there and I'll go for help."

But Dave wouldn't budge. He'd started eating
the bottom of the rainbow glitter avalanche.
Mira didn't even know if glitter was edible.
But that had never stopped Dave before.

Mira nudged Dave with her knees. "Dave,
come on, we've got to get Miss Glitterhorn."

Dave started chomping even more greedily. He
was crushing pebbles in his teeth as he gobbled
the glitter down. His bottom was wiggling as
he moved forward, and he was making happy
snorting noises. Dave and Mira were practically
tunneling into the avalanche now!

"What's happening?!" Jake sounded worried.

"We're just . . . Dave's just . . . eek!"

Dave took one last huge bite of glitter and

backed away. Mira gasped. There was now a

clear path to Jake and Pegasus!

"He's just . . . rescuing you!" Mira stroked Dave's ears and Dave gave a happy burp.

The rain stopped as suddenly as it had started. Jake and Pegasus tiptoed back down the cliff path.

"Are you okay?" asked Mira, as Jake stepped off the dangerous path.

"Yes, I'm fine." Jake still looked pretty pale and shaken.

"Why did you come to pick more glitter when the class was going back?"

Jake shrugged and looked down at his feet. "Some of us have parents who actually expect them to be the best and not to mess absolutely everything up."

Mira didn't know what to say to that, so they

trotted back up the path in silence. Except for Dave's sparkly burps.

∪∪∪

Mira and Jake caught up with their class on the other side of the tree trunks.

"Where on earth have you been?" asked Miss Glitterhorn, as she was counting the students.

Mira looked at Jake, who had an expression of panic on his face.

"Dave and Pegasus both really needed to poop," said Mira.

"Right. Thank you for the detail, Mira. Now let's get back to school."

Once they'd made it through the forest and back to school, everyone hurried into the stables

to dry themselves and their unicorns off. The unicorns settled into their stables for a snack and a nap. Mira, Raheem, and Darcy were told to write "I must not escape detention" one hundred times each before the quest party. The rest of Class Red went to change into dry clothes.

Mira could hear Jake boasting about how much glitter he'd collected as they made their way inside. She passed him in the corridor and Jake stopped talking and blushed.

"What was that about?" asked Darcy.

"Oh, I dunno," said Mira. "Come on, let's get ready for the party."

CHAPTER TEN
Party Time

Mira was upset that she wouldn't be getting a medal in her very first quest ceremony. But she couldn't be too sad when the preparations were so much fun! The unicorns needed to be groomed and glitter-shoed, and the students had to put their rainbow T-shirts on.

That afternoon, Class Red filed out onto the paddock with their unicorns. The entire school was waiting and cheering for them. The knitted mural of the Great Quest of 1488 was back up and there were sparkly flags everywhere.

Class Red sat down in a row at the front.
The school staff were sitting on a platform, and
there was something really tall and big hidden
under a golden curtain.

Madame Shetland got up on the sparkly
mounting block and clapped for silence.

"It is a very special day. Class Red has been
on their first quest."

The whole school cheered.

"They did a lot of glitter picking and
successfully filled the Great Horn!"

Madame Shetland nodded to Colin the
caretaker, who pulled the golden curtain away
to reveal a giant, glittery, curved, upside-down
unicorn horn. Everyone gasped!

"And I am thrilled to announce that the very special extra medal for Most Glitter Collected on Class Red's first quest goes to Flo. She picked seventeen boxes of glitter AND brought back another two boxes' worth in her hair and on her clothes. Such dedication to glitter picking," said Madame Shetland.

The entire school burst into applause. Flo skipped up to the stage to collect her medal, leaving a trail of glittery footprints on the way.

Madame Shetland clapped her hands again. "Marvelous! Class Red, you may now come up to receive your medals for completing the first quest!"

Class Red got up to collect their medals from the stage. Freya, Tamsin, and Seb all

whooped as they were presented with theirs.
Jake even did a bow. Mira, Raheem, and Darcy
stayed in the audience, feeling a bit gloomy.
When Madame Shetland gestured to them to
come and collect their medals, Miss Glitterhorn
spoke loudly so that everyone could hear.
"Madame Shetland, these three students left
detention without permission to join the quest.
Therefore, they will not be receiving any medals."

Madame Shetland frowned. "That is very
unfortunate. But the School Rules are clear:
number 11 . . ."

"No Quest, No Medal," said Mira sadly.

Just then, someone coughed from the stage.
Mira looked around to see where the cough

had come from. Then, to her surprise, Jake started speaking.

"Miss," he said, softly at first, "they did escape detention—"

"All right, Jake, don't rub it in!" Darcy shouted at him.

"They did escape," Jake repeated, speaking louder now, "but it was only because they were worried about us. And actually, Mira saved me on the way back. I'd . . . gotten lost. They . . . they should get medals, too. Maybe just small ones."

Jake's cheeks were red and he was frowning and looking very uncomfortable.

Madame Shetland thought for a moment.

"This is very noble. But they did not complete

the quest and they did leave detention without

permission. That is *very* naughty."

Darcy squeezed Mira's hand.

"However," said Madame Shetland, "their

behavior ultimately enabled them to help a fellow student. So, Mira, Raheem, and Darcy, will you please come up to the stage to receive your medals for . . . Being Cautious and Concerned for One's Fellow Students."

The whole school started clapping and cheering. Mira even thought she could hear Rani yelling her name in the crowd.

They gave one another high fives as they got off the stage. "Medals for being cautious, hey? Your dad will be so proud, Raheem!" said Darcy.

"He really will!" Raheem beamed.

"I'm sorry I got us into more trouble," said Mira. "But I had the best time with you guys. Friendship really is the best kind of magic."

And I finally *got a medal*, Mira thought, as she stroked it happily.

The party was AMAZING. There were cupcakes
and balloons and *glitter* everywhere.

There were bumper cars, a bouncy castle, and a
ball toss. And a long line for the Great Horn.

This was the highlight of the party for
the unicorns, because it made their

horns super sparkly, which is what
makes unicorns happiest.

Each student and their unicorn
stood under the upside-down
horn, and when they were
ready, Miss Hind pulled a rope

and the horn released a shower of glitter onto the pair.

Speaking of unicorns, Mira hadn't seen Dave since the medal ceremony. She started looking for him in the crowd. Then there was a snort behind her.

"Dave! There you are—oh!" Mira stopped, shocked.

Dave was wearing the chewed-up crown she had made for him. He'd put glitter in his mane and was wearing what looked like . . . gold mascara?

He was carrying a picture in his mouth. He'd dressed up as Princess Delilah Sparklehoof! Mira felt like she might cry with happiness. Then she laughed and gave Dave a massive hug.

"Oh, Dave! Did you throw up the crown and everything?"

He nodded.

Mira gave him a kiss. "Thank you."

Mira led Dave to the cupcake table and held out the punch bowl for him to slurp. She looked around. She saw her new friends and their unicorns. She saw their quest medals and then looked at her own special medal. Nothing was quite as she'd expected at Unicorn School, but she wouldn't change a single thing.

Dave did a big poop next to the treats table.

Well, she might change one *or two* little things. Mira quickly dragged Dave away before anyone noticed.

"Come on, Dave, you need some more glitter."
Mira led him over to the Great Horn for their
photo. "You're not what I expected, Dave,"
she said, "but you're one special unicorn."

As the glitter rained down on them,
Mira realized that she had had the best time.
And she couldn't wait to have more amazing
adventures with Dave the unicorn!

WHO IS YOUR UNICORN BEST FRIEND FOREVER (UBFF)?

Answer these questions to find out who your UBFF is!

1. If you were having a unicorn sleepover, what would you and your unicorn BFF do all night?
   a. Sing karaoke, make up fabulous dance routines, and take selfies.
   b. Go on a daring midnight adventure.
   c. Make friendship bracelets!
   d. Eat and sleep.

2. What would be your favorite class at Unicorn School?
   a. Drama. You like to be the star of the show!
   b. PE. You like to be super fit and ready for quests.
   c. History. You love learning about amazing unicorns of the past.
   d. Lunch.

3. What makes you laugh the most?
   a. Surprises. BOO! Ha ha ha ha.
   b. Winning!
   c. You and your BFF giggle all day!
   d. Farts.

4. If you could have a superpower, what would it be?
   a. You'd rather be a celebrity!
   b. Flying, so you could SAVE people from DANGER.
   c. You would give super hugs to make everyone you met super happy.
   d. Invisibility, so you could sneakily eat as many doughnuts and treats as you wanted.

Answers: If you got . . .

Mostly As: Just like STAR, you love the limelight and live your life to be as fabulous as possible.

Mostly Bs: You and BRAVE are made for each other. You're always up for a challenge!

Mostly Cs: It's hard to imagine anyone as loving and giving as PRINCESS, but that's you. You're kind and are always looking out for your friends.

Mostly Ds: Were you ever in any doubt? Your UBFF is DAVE. You're funny, friendly, and completely true to yourself, no matter what the situation.

UNICORN JOKES

Knock, knock.
Who's there?
U.
U who?
Unicorn!

Which unicorn smells?
The poo–nicorn

Which unicorn trains the hardest?
The choo-choo-nicorn

What is a unicorn's favorite type of story?
A fairy tail

What do you call a unicorn without a horn?
Pointless

Where do sick unicorns go?
The horsepital

What's a unicorn's favorite hairstyle?
A ponytail

Dave and Mira's adventures are far from over!
Everyone's favorite unicorn best friends
tackle sports in *Dave the Unicorn: Team Spirit*.

Turn the page for a sneak peek!

CHAPTER ONE
Back to Unicorn School

Mira Desai had been in the kitchen since five A.M. doing her homework.

Usually this would be a very strange thing to do, but Mira's homework was for Unicorn School and was much more fun than normal homework, so she wanted to spend every spare moment she had on it. The students had been asked to make a present for their unicorn, and Mira had thought of the PERFECT present for her unicorn, Dave. She was making him a lunch box. Dave loved lunch. And breakfast . . . and dinner!

Dave wasn't everyone's idea of the perfect unicorn—and he wasn't what Mira had been expecting when she'd dreamed of going to Unicorn School. He was plump, with stumpy little legs and a mane like straw that stuck up in all directions. And Dave was a little naughty. And lazy. And greedy. But NO ONE could make Mira laugh like Dave could—AND he was her UBFF (Unicorn Best Friend Forever). Nothing could change that.

Right now she was decorating the special lunch box with pictures of all the fun they'd had on her last trip to Unicorn School.

Mira was just writing Dave's name in glitter

when her sister, Rani, joined her in the kitchen.
Rani was two years older than Mira and also
went to Unicorn School. She was in Class Yellow,
while Mira was in Class Red. (The classes went
up through all the colors of the rainbow.) Rani's
unicorn was named Angelica, and Rani always
went on and on about how special and sparkly
she was and how they'd won lots of medals. Rani
laid a piece of paper on the table and put her
fluffy pencil case next to it. She was making a
poster to go on Angelica's stall door. She started
carefully drawing her unicorn with a gel pen.

"I'm just drawing a picture of the time
Angelica and I won THREE medals in ONE
DAY," Rani announced.

Mira looked at the side of the lunch box.
She had stuck on a picture of the time Dave had
eaten three cakes in one minute.

"What's that?" said Rani, leaning over. "It looks
like a blob eating some other blobs. And why
have you drawn a rat?"

"That's ME," said Mira angrily.

Rani continued, "It's actually easier for you,
you know. Everyone is SO jealous of me having
a perfect unicorn. But no one would want your
unicorn—everyone knows he's the naughtiest,
awfulest unicorn in the world."

Mira shook her head. Rani had *no* idea about
the adventures she'd had with Dave. They'd made
it all the way through the Fearsome Forest AND

performed a daring rescue on the Mystical Danger Cliff. Mira turned to her sister. "*Awfulest* isn't a word," she said.

They kept drawing in silence. A little later, Mira and Rani's mom and dad came downstairs. "It's so wonderful that they have this experience to share," said Dad.

Then Mira grabbed Rani's pink gel pen and Rani put Mira in a headlock, so Mom had to separate them. She told them to get their bags and get in the car—it was time to go back to Unicorn School!

∪∪∪

Mira was so excited that she could hardly keep still as they drove to the Magic Portal that would take them back to Unicorn School. It wasn't just that she would get to see Dave, but she'd also get to see her new Unicorn School friends Darcy and Raheem, too. The three of them had become great friends in their first semester at Unicorn School, when they'd all gone on a special quest to rescue their classmates.

Mom's car pulled up in the rec center parking lot, and the two girls immediately leaped out and ran over to the bush that hid the Magic Portal. Mom followed behind, carrying their bags, their homework, and one of Mira's shoes.

"You might need these!" she said.

"Thanks, Mom," said Mira, as Rani jumped up and down, impatient to go into the portal. Mira's hands were shaking, and she almost couldn't tie the laces on her sneakers. Mira had gotten brand-new glitter sneakers for her birthday from her parents. She LOVED them, and she couldn't wait to show them to Dave. (Even though Rani said Mira had copied her, since Rani had gotten *her* glitter sneakers first.)

After hugging Mom goodbye and taking the obligatory "off to school" photo, the two sisters crawled into the bush toward a patch of shimmering light. And after Rani told Mira to "stop hogging the portal," they reached out toward the sparkles and tumbled forward, into what felt like thin air. It had only been a few weeks since Mira had last done this, but she'd forgotten how fast it was! It was like going down the big slide at a water park, but with air whooshing around you and rainbow lights whizzing past. Mira and Rani giggled and held on to each other as they shot through the air and landed with a soft *thump* on the Landing Haystack, in front of the Great Hall.

"Bye!" said Rani, running off.

"MIRA!" came a shriek, and Mira turned to see Darcy. Darcy shouted, "Woo-hoo!" and fluffed her big curly hair, then gave Mira a jazz-hand high five. Raheem was behind her, looking a little anxious as he always did, but pleased to see Mira.

"We've been waiting for you to arrive

before we go and get our unicorns!"

Raheem said, grinning.

That gave Mira a happy, warm feeling inside. Although she had friends in the real world, it was so nice to have special friends at Unicorn School to share lots of adventures with! The three friends started to talk about the presents they had made for their unicorns.

"I made this for Brave," said Raheem. "I'm a little worried he won't like it." And he held up a red cape with a blue felt *B* sewn onto it.

"He *will* love that, Raheem—it's so cool!" Mira said.

"I got Star a wig so that we can have matching hair," said Darcy.

As they approached the Grand Paddock, they heard a loud neigh and the thundering of hooves. Raheem's unicorn, Brave, was galloping toward them. Raheem instinctively dived behind a trough just as Brave skidded to a halt. Brave was confused for a moment, but then Raheem quickly crawled out and gave him a hug. Mira was right— Brave LOVED the gift. Raheem put it on him, and Brave stomped around, striking superhero poses.

Darcy and her unicorn, Star, were busy taking selfies with their matching hair. Mira looked around for Dave, until she saw a very familiar unicorn butt poking out from the fence surrounding the stables. Dave had gotten stuck in the fence trying to get to a pile of apples stacked outside the cafeteria. When he heard Mira call his name, he whinnied. So Mira ran over. She tried pulling his legs to help get him out, but he remained stuck in the fence. She climbed over and gave him a shove from the other side.

With a loud *POP*, Dave came free from the fence and fell backward, knocking over a unicorn who'd been walking past.

"Sorry!" called Mira, as the unicorn picked herself up, tutted at Dave, and trotted away.

Mira turned back to her unicorn, who was trotting straight back toward the gap in the fence, eyeing the apples hungrily.

"Wait—Dave, I got you something!" said Mira, pulling the lunch box out of her bag.

Dave's eyes went wide and he gave a happy grunt. He was even more delighted when he nudged the lid off with his nose and saw that Mira had filled the lunch box with doughnuts. He scarfed them down immediately,

just as Mira

had expected

he would,

but he did a little trick of bouncing each doughnut on his nose before catching it in his mouth, which made Mira laugh.

"I don't think people realize how clever you are," said Mira, scratching behind his ears. Being back at Unicorn School was . . .

THE BEST!

Dave the Unicorn: Team Spirit is out now, wherever books are sold! And keep an eye out for book three, *Dave the Unicorn: Dance Party!*

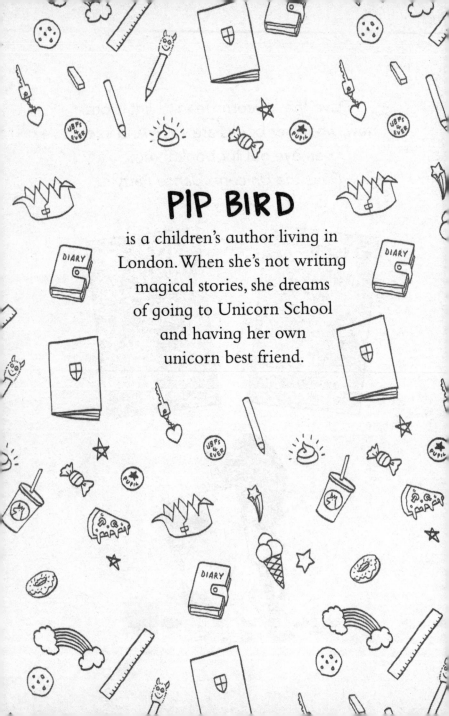

PIP BIRD

is a children's author living in London. When she's not writing magical stories, she dreams of going to Unicorn School and having her own unicorn best friend.